Andrew's Marble

By Katie Machoskie   Illustrated By Libby Carruth Krock

AuthorHouse™
1663 Liberty Drive, Suite 200
Bloomington, IN 47403
www.authorhouse.com
Phone: 1-800-839-8640

First published by AuthorHouse 1/7/2008

ISBN: 978-1-4343-4167-9 (sc)

Library of Congress Control Number: 2007910178

Printed in the United States of America
Bloomington, Indiana

This book is printed on acid-free paper.

authorHOUSE®

For Andrew with love.

Click! Clack! Whoosh!
Whirrrrrrrrrr, Clack! Clack!! Clack!!!
Andrew peeked out from his covers just as Stormy,
his kitten, batted his lucky, cobalt-blue marble off his
nightstand with her tiny, white paw. He watched it
bounce along his wooden floor, out his bedroom door
and down the hallway.

Andrew rolled out of bed and landed on his feet.
Today was the first day of second grade.

He brushed his teeth.

He spiked his hair with gel.

He pulled on his new jeans and his favorite
skateboarding shirt.

He grabbed his new, red backpack
and raced downstairs.

"Ooops! Almost forgot,"
he said as he ran back upstairs and stuck his
lucky marble in his pocket.

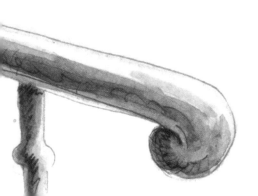

He munched his cereal and gulped his juice.

He grabbed a handful of yellow snapdragons for his
new teacher. He kissed his little brother on top of
his fuzzy, blonde head.

He waved to his mom as he zoomed out the door.
Andrew walked slowly to the bus stop, tossing his
lucky marble up and down in the air.
"1,2,3,4..." Andrew tossed his marble up and down.
"Five times in the air and five perfect catches" he thought.
"Wait 'til I tell Edward."

"6, 7, 8, 9..."
but on the sixteenth toss, the marble
hit the road and started bouncing away.
Boing, boing, clack, clack, clack.
Andrew watched his lucky, cobalt-blue
marble as it started to roll down the hill.
It rolled down a dirt path, over a bridge
and started bouncing again.
Boing, boing, boing!

Andrew groaned as he
watched it roll into a dark cave
under the bridge. He scrambled after it,
but screeched to a stop in front of the cave.

"RRRRRRRRRRRROARRRRRRRRRRR!"
growled a voice from inside the cave.

Andrew jumped. It was the loudest roar he'd ever heard.
He said in a small voice, "Excuse me, but could you please
toss me my marble? It rolled into your cave."

"RRRRRRRROARRRRRRRRRRRRRRRR!"
said the voice.
Andrew wrinkled his nose. Every time the thing in the cave
roared, the most horrible smell came out.
It smelled like his street the time the garbage men
forgot to pick up the trash last August.
Then Andrew remembered that Edward's older brother
told him that a mean dragon lived in this cave.
He didn't believe him. Until now.
Edward's brother said that the dragon looked like black,
slimey seaweed and never took a bath.

Peeeeeeeeee-U! Edward's brother was right!

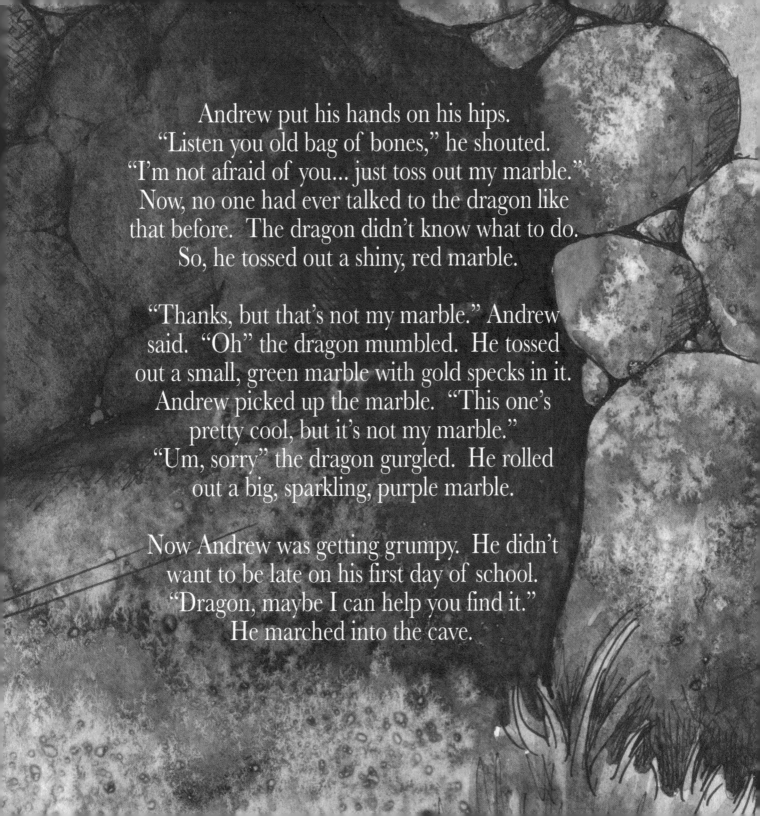

Andrew put his hands on his hips.
"Listen you old bag of bones," he shouted.
"I'm not afraid of you... just toss out my marble."
Now, no one had ever talked to the dragon like
that before. The dragon didn't know what to do.
So, he tossed out a shiny, red marble.

"Thanks, but that's not my marble." Andrew
said. "Oh" the dragon mumbled. He tossed
out a small, green marble with gold specks in it.
Andrew picked up the marble. "This one's
pretty cool, but it's not my marble."
"Um, sorry" the dragon gurgled. He rolled
out a big, sparkling, purple marble.

Now Andrew was getting grumpy. He didn't
want to be late on his first day of school.
"Dragon, maybe I can help you find it."
He marched into the cave.

"Ahhhhhhhhhhhhhhhh!" Andrew gasped.
Once he was inside the cave, all he saw were marbles!
He stepped over a row of orange marbles. He
tip-toed over a pile of pink ones and almost slipped on
three rows of yellow marbles. He turned around and
saw silver marbles stuck in the wall of the cave.
Cat's-eye marbles peeked out of rocks and a large
circle of black ones were piled into a hole
in the cave's floor.

In the middle of the cave was the biggest, black dragon Andrew had ever seen. (Actually, it was the only dragon he'd ever seen...except in movies.) Wedged between the dragon's horns sat Andrew's lucky cobalt-blue marble. It must have rolled onto the dragon's head while he was taking a nap!

Andrew looked at the dragon.
"Where did you get all these marbles?"
The dragon looked around the cave.
"They just roll in when people lose them. No one
has ever asked for them back. Until today."

Andrew couldn't believe it.
"I'm the only one who has ever come
looking for their marble?"
The dragon looked sad.
"Everyone is afraid of me."

"Well," said Andrew, "maybe you shouldn't growl so loud." Then Andrew pinched his nose. "And maybe you should take a bath once in awhile." The dragon had big, hot dragon tears in his eyes.
"Do I smell that bad? I can't smell anything."
Andrew started to laugh. The dragon began to cry.
"Go away. It's not nice to laugh at me."

Andrew patted the dragon
on his sticky head.

"I'm sorry dragon. You have two
huge, green marbles stuck in your
nose! No wonder you can't smell!
Here, let me help you!"

Andrew began to tickle the dragon's
nose with one of the flowers he had
for his teacher. The dragon sneezed
three times and it sounded just like
thunder. The marbles shot out of the
dragon's nose, hit a wall and bounced
out of the cave.

Andrew giggled. The dragon began to laugh.
Andrew put his arm around the dragon.

"I really want my marble back. If you promise to take a bath
while I'm at school, I'll come back and we can play."
"Why would you want to do that?" the dragon asked.
Andrew sighed. "Because that's what friends do.
They play together."
"Oh. OK" the dragon whispered.

Andrew scooped up his backpack.
"My name is Andrew. What's your name?"
The dragon looked at him.
"Why do you want to know my name?"
Andrew rolled his eyes. "Well, duh! That's what friends do.
They call each other by their names."

The dragon had to think for a long time.
"My mom used to call me Garth," he said hopefully.

"OK Garth, I'm going to get my marble.
It's stuck in your horns."
Andrew put one foot on the dragon's horn and his other
foot on Garth's nose.

He tugged.

He grunted.

Finally, the marble popped out of Garth's horns.
"Thanks Garth! See you after school!"

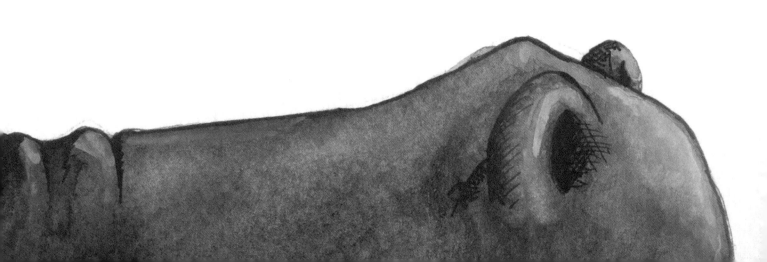

Andrew ran over the bridge,
up the hill
and stopped at the bus stop
just as the big yellow bus drove up.

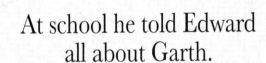

At school he told Edward
all about Garth.

Andrew read a book, did his math,
played capture the flag at recess,
ate pizza (because Mondays were
always pizza days) and watched
the hands of the clock go
Tick, Tick, Tick.

When the afternoon
bell rang, he raced to the bus,
jumped off at his stop and ran down
the hill, over the bridge and slid at the
front of the cave like it was first base.
He rolled his lucky cobalt-blue
marble into the cave.

"Roar?" said Garth.

Inside the cave, Garth was waiting with a big, toothy smile. His green dragon skin sparkled from the long bath he had taken in the lake while Andrew was at school.

"Wow Garth! You clean up great!" said Andrew. (That's what his mom always said to his dad when they went out to dinner.)

Andrew and Garth
played with the silver, purple, green
and, of course, Andrew's lucky,
cobalt-blue marble.
Sometimes Edward would play with them
and they'd have a marble tournament.
They played together whenever they could
and stayed friends forever.

Because that's
what friends do.